# Wildfires

Ted O'Hare

Bethany, Missouri

Photo Credits:
Cover © P.I.R.;  Title Page © Dale Stork;  Page 4 © Olaru Radian-Alexandru;  Page 5 © Paul Senyszyn;  Page 6 ©
Darin Echelberger;  Page 7 © Dale Stork;  Page 9 © Ali Mazraie Shadi, Breezeart;  Page 10 © Wesley Aston;
Page 11 © Marylin;  Page 12 © John Cairns;  Page 13 © Jhaz Photography;  Page 14 © Kubilay Tanrikulu;
Page 15 © Bob McMillan/ FEMA Photo;  Page 16 © Millsrymer;  Page 17 © Jean-Joseph Renucci, DOD;  Page 18
© Andrea Booher/FEMA Photo;  Page 19 © Mike Norton, Andrea Booher/FEMA Photo;  Pages 20, 21 ©
Bob McMillan/ FEMA Photo;  Page 22 © Constantgardener

Cataloging-in-Publication Data

O'Hare, Ted, 1961-
    Wildfires / Ted O'Hare. — 1st ed.
    p. cm. — (Natural disasters)

    Includes bibliographical references and index.
    Summary:  Illustrations and text introduce wildfires, from
how fires start, to what a wildfire is, firefighting, prescribed fires,
and more.
    ISBN-13:  978-1-4242-1405-1 (lib. bdg. : alk. paper)
    ISBN-10:  1-4242-1405-X (lib. bdg. : alk. paper)
    ISBN-13:  978-1-4242-1495-2 (pbk. : alk. paper)
    ISBN-10:  1-4242-1495-5 (pbk. : alk. paper)

    1. Wildfires—Juvenile literature.  2. Fires—Juvenile literature.
3. Fire ecology—Juvenile literature.
[1. Wildfires.  2. Fires.  3. Fire ecology.  4. Natural disasters.]
I. O'Hare, Ted, 1961-  II. Title.  III. Series.
    SD421.23.O43 2007
    363.37'9—dc22

First edition
© 2007 Fitzgerald Books
802 N. 41st Street, P.O. Box 505
Bethany, MO  64424, U.S.A.
Printed in China
Library of Congress Control Number:  2006911294

# Table of Contents

# What Is a Fire?

Fire is one of our most important tools. Fires help us keep warm, cook our food, and provide light to see. But fire is also one of our most destructive forces.

Fires can happen outdoors. Fires can also happen inside buildings.

No matter where they occur, fires cause damage and may even kill people. People may die either because of smoke **inhalation** or burns.

Fires begin when **fuel** is mixed with oxygen and heat. For instance, trees in a forest can provide the fuel. The air provides oxygen. And a lighted match or cigarette, dropped on the ground, provides the heat.

## Things Needed for Fire

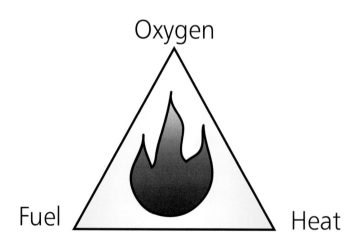

Oxygen

Fuel

Heat

# Wildfires

Wildfires burn in natural settings. Some are caused by lightning. And some are started by humans. Often huge areas of trees are destroyed when fires burn out of control.

Fires can burn slow or fast. Fast-burning fires are often driven by winds and dry conditions. This helps the fire spread and grow out of control.

13

# Fighting Fires

Many fires today happen in the western part of the country, where dry conditions exist. Lack of rain is the main reason why many fires start.

Firefighters risk their lives to help put out fires.

Helicopters and planes are used to fight wildfires. The pilot flies over the fire and drops water or **fire retardant** to put out the flames.

Water

Fire Retardant

Hotshot crews are workers trained to be the first to arrive at fires. Their job is to try to put out the flames.

Some firefighters even set fires. **Prescribed fires** are controlled fires. Prescribed fires burn leaves and branches on the ground and help stop bigger fires.

# Benefits of Fires

Fire is important in maintaining a healthy **ecosystem**. A fire allows room for new plants to grow. **Ash**, which is left by fires, provides rich minerals for new plants.

# Glossary

**ash** (ASH) — solid matter that is left when something burns

**ecosystem** (EE koh sis tum) — a community of plants and animals

**fire retardant** (FIRE  rih TAR dunt) — a mixture of chemicals that slows down a fire

**fuel** (FYOO uhl) — material that can burn

**inhalation** (in huh LAY shun) — breathing something in

**prescribed fires** (PRE skrybd  FIREZ) — fires that are set on purpose

# Index

**FURTHER READING**

Hamilton, John. *Wildfires.* Abdo & Daughters, 2005.
Morrison, Taylor. *Wildfire.* Houghton Mifflin, 2006.

**WEBSITES TO VISIT**

Because Internet links change so often, Fitzgerald Books has developed an online list of websites related to the subject of this book. This site is updated regularly. Please use this link to access the list:  www.fitzgeraldbookslinks.com/nd/wil

**ABOUT THE AUTHOR**

Ted O'Hare is an author and editor of children's nonfiction books. Ted has written over fifty children's books over the past decade. Ted has worked for many publishing houses including the Macmillan Children's Book Group.